Disney
Winnie the Pooh

Tales of Adventure
Treasury

Bath · New York · Cologne · Melbourne · Delhi
Hong Kong · Shenzhen · Singapore · Amsterdam

This edition published by Parragon Books Ltd in 2015

Parragon Books Ltd
Chartist House
15–17 Trim Street
Bath BA1 1HA, UK
www.parragon.com

Written by Catherine Hapka
'Don't Be Roo-diculous' written by Thea Feldman
Illustrated by the Disney Storybook Artists

ISBN 978-1-4723-5131-9

Printed in China

Contents

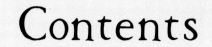

Better than Honey

"Good morning," Winnie the Pooh said to himself with a yawn. "What shall I do today?"

Pooh thought about his question as he climbed out of bed. By the time he'd finished doing his stoutness exercises, he'd come up with an answer.

"I believe it would be a fine day for some honey," he said.

Feeling pleased with his decision, Pooh went to his
cupboard. There were several honeypots on the shelves.
But there was no honey inside any of them.

"Oh, bother," Pooh said. "I forgot that I ate all of
my honey yesterday."

Pooh's tummy **grumbled**. Pooh leaned closer to listen to it.

"What's that?" he said. "You say we should go and visit Rabbit?

What a wonderful idea! He always has plenty of honey."

"Good morning, Rabbit," Pooh said politely. "Have you had breakfast yet?"

Rabbit looked suspicious. "Yes, I have," he said. "Haven't you?"

"Why, no. I haven't. Thank you for inviting me," Pooh said.

"Did I?" Rabbit looked rather confused. "Well, then I suppose you'd better come in."

Soon, Pooh was enjoying a smackerel of honey. "I never tasted such delicious honey," he said in a sticky voice.

"I never knew someone so obsessed with honey." Rabbit sounded a bit cross. "Don't you ever do anything but eat honey, Pooh Bear?"

Pooh stopped eating. "I suppose I must do other things sometimes, mustn't I?" Pooh said. "The trouble is, I can't quite think of what those things might be just now."

"Well, there's no more honey," Rabbit said.

"Oh, dear," Pooh said. "Well, what are you going to do now, Rabbit? Because perhaps I could do the same thing."

"I'm going to work in my garden," Rabbit answered.

Pooh didn't know much about gardening.
But he agreed to give it a try. First he helped
Rabbit pick some carrots.

Then they watered the peas.

After that, it was time to **mulch** the tomatoes.

Pooh enjoyed all of it. It wasn't the same as eating honey. But it was fun to try something different.

"That's enough gardening, Pooh," Rabbit said after a while.

"Why don't you go and find something else to do?"

"Like eating honey?" Pooh said hopefully. "Is there any more?"

"No," Rabbit replied. "You'll have to think of something else."

CABEGE

Pooh wandered off, thinking as hard as he could.

Then he noticed that he was near Owl's house.

"Owl is the wisest friend I have," Pooh said to himself.

"Perhaps he'll be able to help me figure out what to do now."

Owl listened to Pooh's dilemma. "This puts me in mind of my great-aunt Phyllis," he said. "She loved trying new things. Knitting, baking, draughts, camel racing, fly fishing ..."

Owl went on and on and on. Pooh tried to keep up with what he was saying. But the words piled up far too quickly for a bear of very little brain to follow.

Finally Owl stopped talking. "So, which of those interesting things would you suggest I try, Owl?" Pooh asked politely.

Owl peered at him in surprise. "Weren't you listening, Pooh?" he asked. "Aunt Phyllis told me she was never so happy as when she was writing her memoirs. You ought to do that."

Owl gave Pooh some paper and a pencil and sent him on his way. Pooh sat down and began to write.

He was working hard when Eeyore wandered by.

"Hello, Pooh," Eeyore said gloomily. "What are you doing?"

"Writing my memoirs," Pooh said. "It was Owl's idea."

"That sounds interesting," Eeyore said.

"What are you doing, Eeyore?" Pooh asked.

Eeyore sighed. "Going to the thistle patch for lunch."

Pooh's tummy **rumbled**. "Is it lunchtime already?"

He thought about stopping by Rabbit's house for some tasty honey. But thinking about Rabbit reminded Pooh that he was supposed to be trying new things today.

"May I join you, Eeyore?" he asked. "Thistles for lunch sounds like a delicious new thing to try."

"It does?" Eeyore said doubtfully.

"Well?" Eeyore asked Pooh. "How do you like the thistles?"

"They're, er, different," Pooh said politely, picking a prickly bit of thistle out of his tongue. "They'd probably be even tastier with a smackerel of honey."

Just then, Tigger bounced into view. "Hoo-hoo-hoo!" he cried when he saw Pooh. "What's new, Buddy Bear?"

"A lot," Pooh said. "I'm trying interesting new things today."

"You are?" Tigger said. "Then how's about you try some bouncing? It's the *abso-tively* most *inneresting* thing there is!"

"It is?" Pooh said. "Then I suppose I should try it."

Pooh and Tigger **bounced** together for a while.

"Whaddaya think, Buddy Bear?" Tigger said.

"It's very interesting," Pooh replied breathlessly,

"but rather tiring. And it does make one a bit hungry."

They bounced towards Piglet's house. "Watch this!" Tigger told Pooh. "Hello, Piglet!"

He bounced Piglet right off his feet. "H-hello, Tigger," Piglet said. "Hello, Pooh. What are you two doing?"

"Bouncing! Hoo-hoo-hoo-hoo!" Tigger bounced so high that he bounced right out of sight.

Pooh stopped bouncing. "I'm trying new things today, Piglet," he said. "Can you think of anything I should try?"

"You could help me collect haycorns," Piglet suggested.

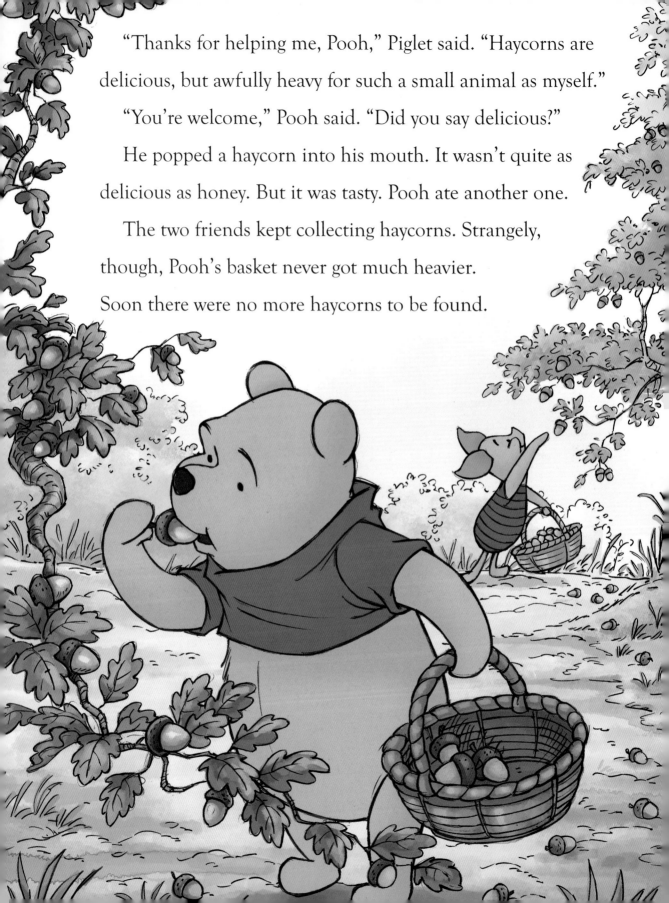

"Thanks for helping me, Pooh," Piglet said. "Haycorns are delicious, but awfully heavy for such a small animal as myself."

"You're welcome," Pooh said. "Did you say delicious?"

He popped a haycorn into his mouth. It wasn't quite as delicious as honey. But it was tasty. Pooh ate another one.

The two friends kept collecting haycorns. Strangely, though, Pooh's basket never got much heavier.

Soon there were no more haycorns to be found.

"Thank you, Pooh," Piglet said again. "Would you like to come in for tea? I think I have enough haycorns for us both."

"No thank you, Piglet." Pooh paused to let out a polite burp. "I don't seem to be hungry right now. At least not for haycorns."

Pooh went in search of something else to do. He soon came upon little Roo playing in the sandpit.

"Hello, Pooh," Roo said. "Want to build sand sculptures with me?"

"That sounds like an interesting new thing to try," Pooh agreed, joining Roo in the sandpit.

The two of them made several sand sculptures.

"This is almost as much fun as eating

honey!" Pooh said.

HUNNY

Pooh and Piglet played together in the sand until Kanga appeared. "Bath time, Roo," she said.

"Aw, do I have to, Mama?" Roo asked.

"Bath time sounds interesting," Pooh said. "Can I try it, too?"

Kanga sized him up uncertainly. "I'm not sure you and the water will both fit in the tub, Pooh," she said. "But if you want something to do, you could wash the soup pot for me."

"All right," Pooh said. "That sounds interesting, too."

It turned out that Kanga knew about lots of interesting new things Pooh could try, such as **sweeping** the step,

stirring the porridge,

carrying in some apples for supper and much more.

He was hanging the laundry out to dry when Christopher Robin
appeared. "Hello, Pooh Bear," the boy said. "What have you been
up to today?"

"Oh, all sorts of things." Pooh told Christopher Robin about
his day. "Some things I tried made me more hungry and some
made me less hungry." Pooh sighed. "But I'm afraid all of them
made me think about honey."

Christopher Robin laughed. "Silly old bear," he said. "Of course they did! Pooh Bears are meant to eat honey."

Pooh felt confused. "So I shouldn't try new things after all?"

"No, it's good to try new things," the boy said. "Otherwise, how would you know how much you liked your old things?"

"Shall we go and find some honey then?" Pooh asked.

"That sounds like the best idea you've had all day," Christopher Robin agreed.

Bounce with
Me!

Tigger loved to bounce.

He bounced in the morning. He bounced in the evening. He bounced all day in between.

But that was no surprise. After all, bouncing was what tiggers did best.

One day, Tigger was in a hurry to reach one of his favourite bouncing spots. He was too impatient to bounce all the way to the bridge and then bounce across it. Instead, he just bounced right over the stream!

"Hoo-hoo-hoo-hoo!" he cried.

"I just invented a new game! A *superiffic* one!

Which isn't all that surprising – since inventing

games is what tiggers do best!"

Tigger couldn't wait to tell his friends about his new game.
He bounced back across the stream – and landed on Eeyore's house.

"Guess what?" Tigger said. "I just invented a new bouncing game.
It's called, uh …" He paused to think.

"Take your time," Eeyore said with a sigh. "I wasn't doing
anything important anyway."

"It's called 'bounce over the brook'!" Tigger finished at last.
"BOB for short."

"I'm the best BOB player ever!" Tigger went on. "Betcha can't beat me!"

"I bet you're right," Eeyore agreed gloomily. "I'm not much of a bouncer."

"Just give it a try," Tigger said. "One little bounce?"

Eeyore tried to bounce. But his feet hardly left the ground.

"*That's* what you call a bounce?" Tigger exclaimed. "Clearly bouncing is NOT what eeyores do best!"

Eeyore sighed again. "Told you so."

Since Eeyore couldn't play with him, Tigger bounced over to Pooh's house. Pooh and Piglet were there, sharing some honey.

"Hello!" Tigger cried, bouncing Pooh right off his feet ... and a honeypot right on to Piglet's head!

"Hello, Tigger," Pooh said. "Care for a smackerel of honey?"

"Tiggers do *not* like honey," Tigger said. "But they do like playing BOB."

"Bob?" Piglet said, confused. "Who's that?"

"It's not a *who*, it's a *what*. Come on! I'll show you!"
Tigger bounced off without waiting for a reply.

Pooh and Piglet followed Tigger to the stream, where Tigger explained his new game.

"You just bounce over – like this!" He demonstrated ten or eleven times. "Give it a try, Buddy Bear!"

Pooh had **never really** bounced before. But Tigger made it look like **fun.**

Pooh bent his knees. He swung his arms.

He pushed off....

Splash!

Pooh sat up. He hadn't made it across the stream.
He was *in* the stream, feeling like a Soggy Bear
of Great Dampness.

"Bouncing is NOT what
pooh bears do best,"
Tigger declared.

"Your turn," Tigger told Piglet. "Let's see your best bounce!"

"Oh, dear." Piglet sounded nervous. "I don't think this is a very good idea."

"I think you're right, Piglet," Pooh agreed as he climbed out of the stream. "Bouncing is much harder than it looks."

"We'd better go and get you dried off, Pooh," Piglet said.

"Hey, wait!" Tigger cried.

But it was too late. Pooh and Piglet were gone.
Tigger's shoulders drooped. "I guess bouncing
isn't what piglets do best, either," he mumbled.

Then he had an idea.

"Aha!" Tigger cried. "I bet Ol' Long Ears will bounce with me. His feet are made for it!" He bounced away to Rabbit's house.

"Oh, good grief, not you again!" Rabbit said when he saw Tigger.

"I see you came to bounce my garden to smithereens!"

"Nope," Tigger said. "I came to invite you to play BOB with me."

"I don't have time for any of your silly games, Tigger,"

Rabbit said. "I have too much work to do! Now shoo!"

Tigger could tell that Rabbit wasn't in the mood for bouncing. "Maybe bouncing isn't what rabbits do best after all," he said to himself. "Luckily, I know someone else who lives close by!" He bounced over to Owl's house and knocked on the door.

"Hoo-hoo-hoo-hoo!" he called. "Anybody home?

When Owl answered the door, Tigger told him about BOB.

"What do you say?" he asked. "Want to play?"

"Bob, eh?" Owl said thoughtfully. "Some people used to call

my great-uncle Robert by that name. Speaking of great-uncle

Robert, did I ever tell you about the time ..."

Owl talked.

And talked.

And talked some
more....

An hour later, Owl finally paused for a breath.

"Very *exciterating* story," Tigger said. "Gotta go!"

He bounced away before Owl could say anything else.

Whew! He'd forgotten that telling long stories was
what owls did best. And tiggers did *not* like long stories.

Eventually, Tigger ended up at Kanga's house, hoping to find Roo. Kanga was home baking a cake.

"I'm sorry, dear, but Roo is out playing in the Wood," Kanga said kindly. "I'm not sure when he'll be back, but you can come in and help me bake my cake if you like."

Tigger was excited to help, but when he accidentally bounced Kanga's cake mix right off the table, a thought occurred to him. His bouncing was something his friends did *not* like at all.

Tigger left Kanga's house and bounced towards the stream.
But his bounces kept getting smaller.

And smaller.

And smaller.

Finally they weren't really bounces at all. What was the point?
None of his friends even liked his bouncing. It was no wonder
Tigger couldn't find anyone to play BOB with him.

"A game's not much fun if you've got nobody to play with,"
Tigger muttered. "Feeling lonely is *not* what tiggers do best."

Suddenly Tigger heard laughter coming from just ahead.

"I *recognizize* that laugh," Tigger said. He bounced towards the sound and soon spotted Roo.

"Hi, Tigger!" Roo said.

"Hi, Little Buddy," Tigger said. "Want to do some bouncing? I just invented a great new game!"

Tigger and Roo bounced to the stream and Tigger showed Roo how to play BOB.

"This is great!" Roo cried as he and Tigger bounced from one side of the stream to the other. "Look at me, Tigger. Whee!"

"Hoo-hoo-hoo-hoo!" Tigger cried. "Playing BOB is what tiggers *and* roos do best!"

It was true. Tigger had finally found the perfect friend to bounce with him!

Meanwhile, Tigger's friends gathered and began discussing Tigger's BOB game.

"Well, I think it's a splendid game for Tigger," Owl began.

"It *does* keep him away from my garden," Rabbit admitted.

"The more bouncing Tigger does *outside*, the better," said Kanga with a smile.

"I won't have to keep rebuilding my house," said Eeyore.

"I'll stay much cleaner," Piglet said brightly.

"And I'll stay much drier," added Pooh.

So it was decided ... BOB was just the sort of game that tiggers should play.

Tigger was having such fun that he didn't notice his friends arriving. Suddenly, he heard clapping.

"That was a fine bounce, Tigger," Pooh called out.

"Good show, little Roo," Owl added.

The rest of Tigger's friends were there as well, clapping and cheering, which made Tigger bounce higher than ever. Tigger's friends might not be very good at bouncing. But cheering on their friends? Well, that was what they ALL did best!

Don't Be Roo-diculous!

One sunny afternoon, Roo and Tigger were bouncing together in the Hundred-Acre Wood. They bounced to the left and they bounced to the right. But mostly they bounced up and down. Roo couldn't help but notice that he couldn't bounce as high as his friend.

Roo looked up at a nearby tree. One branch hung lower than the rest. "Let's see who can reach that branch first!" he cried.

"You got it, Little Buddy!" said Tigger.

Roo **Scrunched** up his face and closed his eyes and PUSHED off the ground as hard as he could!

Roo opened his eyes. He saw himself go up, up, up, up.
But he still couldn't get anywhere near the branch. Tigger touched
it easily. When Roo came down, he lost his balance ...

... and landed in a bed of flowers.

"Thinking of picking some flowers for your mama?"
asked Tigger as he helped Roo up.

"I guess," said Roo sadly.

"What's the matter, Little Buddy?" asked Tigger.

"You sure can bounce awfully high," said Roo.

"I wish I could bounce as high as you."

"Don't be *roo-diculous*," said Tigger. "You bounce pretty good for a little fella."

Tigger picked some flowers for Kanga and handed them to Roo. "Besides," he added as he bounced off, "bouncing is what tiggers do best! Ta-ta for now!"

Roo sighed into the flowers. "I wish I weren't so small," he said.

He looked up at the tree. "One day," he said, "I want to reach that

branch and swing from it!"

"Pardon me for interrupting, but perhaps I can help," said

Winnie the Pooh, who was on his way back from Piglet's house.

"Do you really think so, Pooh?" asked Roo, looking at his friend with interest. Perhaps, he thought, Pooh really did know something about how to be bigger.

"Why, yes," said Pooh. He took the flowers out of Roo's arms and lifted up his little friend. Pooh carried Roo until they were underneath the tree branch in question. Then, he held Roo up. Pooh had to stand on his tippytoes and Roo had to s-t-r-e-t-ch his arms as high as they would go ... but it worked! Roo was able to reach the tree branch!

"**Whee!**" cried Roo, as he swung from the branch.

"Thank you so much, Pooh!"

Pooh **stretched** his own arms up high and gave a yawn.

"You're quite welcome," said Pooh. He looked at the tree trunk. "I suppose I can rest here while you play and make sure you get down safely. Just let me know when you're ready, Roo."

No sooner had Pooh's back touched the tree than he fell asleep.
Roo swung happily for a few minutes. Then his arms got tired.
"Oh, Pooh?" he called down.

z z z," was Pooh's response.

Roo didn't want to wake Pooh, so he scrambled up on to the
branch. Now he could swing his legs, which was much easier than
swinging by his arms. Even so, Roo began to grow bored. If I were
bigger, he thought, I could get down by myself!

After what seemed like a long time to Roo, he heard someone
coming. It was Christopher Robin.

Not terribly surprised to find Pooh snoozing against a tree,
Christopher Robin *was* very surprised to find Roo sitting *in*
the tree. Roo explained what had happened.

"I can help you down," said Christopher Robin, who didn't want to wake Pooh either. He held out his arms and Roo jumped safely into them.

Once back on the ground, Roo thanked Christopher Robin. Then he scooped up the flowers and unhappily headed home.

Kanga was delighted with the flowers. "You're so
thoughtful, Little One!" she cried, giving Roo a big hug.

It felt good to be hugged by his mother. But Roo was really still thinking about how he wished he were **bigger**.

He didn't like the feeling of not being able to do things for himself. Things were going to change!

The next day, Kanga announced
she was going to bake apple pies
that afternoon.

Without saying a word to his mother,
Roo headed towards the apple trees.
He was determined to bring back the
plumpest apples he could find.

Roo tried his hardest,
but he just couldn't
ju**m**p high enough
to reach even the
lowest apples.

Roo sat down and rested his head in his hands.

He felt
so
small.

Rabbit nearly ran Roo over with his wagon.

"Roo," he said, a bit irritated, "you're too small to be sitting in the middle of the path like that. Why, anyone could just knock you down before they even see you."

"I'm sorry, Rabbit," said Roo. "I just wanted to pick some apples for my mother."

"Well, why didn't you say so?" said Rabbit, who grabbed his rake and, using its long handle, KNOCKED DOWN several apples before going on his way.

Next, Tigger **bounced** by. He **bounced** into the tree
and brought Roo a whole branchful of apples!
"Hoo-hoo-hoo-hoo!"
cried Tigger. "Apple picking
is what tiggers do best!"

Owl flew by and landed very high up in
the tree. "If it's apples you want," he called,
"here you are!" Then he **flapped** his
wings until several **fell** off the
highest
branches.

Roo was careful to dodge them as they came

d
o
w
n.

Soon Pooh arrived and lifted Roo up again. This was the closest Roo got to picking some apples on his own.

Roo delivered all the apples to a very pleased Kanga. Then he went off to have a good long sulk. Though he wasn't quite sure why, sulking reminded him of Eeyore. Without really planning it, Roo ended up at his friend's house of sticks.

Eeyore wasn't home, so Roo sat down to wait for him to return. Absent-mindedly, he picked up a stick that had fallen from Eeyore's house. As Roo examined it, he began thinking it would be useful for lots of things besides Eeyore's house – a Pooh Sticks stick, a pretend sword ...

Then suddenly Roo had an idea. "That's it!" he cried. "I know just what to do." And he hurried off.

Roo stopped by Rabbit's house and borrowed a hammer and nails. Then he went into the woods and collected as many sticks as he could find.

Roo began to nail sticks to a very TALL tree. Before long, he had a ladder that he could climb to reach the tree branches without anyone's help!

Roo couldn't help but feel rather proud of himself. He resolved to make ladders on several more trees. But for now, he climbed the tree in front of him and happily swung from its branches.

Roo was unaware of how much time had passed, until he heard his mother's worried cry. "Roo!"

Then he heard Rabbit, Owl, Tigger and Pooh calling him, too. "I'm over here!" he shouted.

Everyone quickly gathered by the tree. "Roo!" said Kanga. "How on earth did you get up there?!"

Roo pointed out his ladder. Then he admitted to Kanga and the others how small he had been feeling.

"That's using your noggin!" said Tigger, admiring the ladder. "There's nothing small about your brain, Little Buddy!"

Roo grinned from ear to ear

as he

climbed

down.

"I'm so proud of you, dear," Kanga said. "You didn't give up. You kept at it until you figured out how to feel bigger!

"And don't worry," she added. "You will be bigger soon enough." Kanga lifted a tired little Roo into her pouch. "But for now, you're just the right size!"

Eeyore's
Gloomy Day

It was a cloudy, rather gloomy day in the Hundred-Acre Wood.
At least that was how Eeyore saw it.

Then again, Eeyore always saw the gloomy side of things.
"Looks like rain," he muttered, eyeing a passing cloud. "Probably be
a humdinger of a storm. Lightning, thunder, the works."

Eeyore cocked his head, listening for the **rumble** of thunder. Instead he heard cheerful whistling. A moment later, Winnie the Pooh appeared.

"Hello, Eeyore," Pooh said. "Lovely day, isn't it?"

Eeyore thought about the question. "If you say so, Pooh. Not sure I'd call it that myself. But who cares what I think?"

Pooh scratched his head. He often found Eeyore's comments a bit puzzling. Then again, he found many things puzzling.

"I was just taking a walk," he said. "Would you care to join me?"

"A walk?" Eeyore looked up. "Not sure that's a good idea with the storm coming."

Pooh glanced up. There was only one cloud in sight – a small one that resembled a honeypot. "Er, I'm not sure what kind of idea it is, Eeyore," he said. "I just thought I'd go and visit Piglet and thought you might like to come, too."

Eeyore shrugged. "It's not as if I have anything better to do."

Pooh and Eeyore arrived at Piglet's house to find him with a broom in one hand and a dustpan in the other.

"Oh, dear," Piglet said, sounding rather frantic. "Just when I finish cleaning one bit, another gets dirty again!"

"Never mind, Piglet," Pooh said. "Your house looks very clean to me already."

Piglet shook his head. "Can't you see the dust over there? And the leaves just there and oh, dear, the smudges ..."

"He's right, you know," Eeyore said.

"Dirt's everywhere. On the ground.

Falling out of trees.

Creeps up on you when you're sleeping. Yup. Getting things clean is a full-time job. No time to eat or sleep or frolic about singing tra-la-la. Certainly no time to waste talking to us."

Piglet looked surprised. "I do like to keep things tidy," he said. "But I like visiting friends even more. Thanks for helping me remember that, Eeyore."

"Did I?" Eeyore said. "Hmm. Must've been an accident."

"Speaking of friends," Piglet said, "I told Rabbit I'd stop by for some squash soup."

"Squash soup?" Pooh licked his lips. "Do you suppose he made enough for all of us?"

In fact, Rabbit had made a very large quantity of squash soup. That was good, since Pooh proceeded to eat a very large quantity. Almost all of it, in fact.

"Mmm," Pooh said when he'd finished. "That was very good soup, Rabbit. I don't suppose you have any more?"

"No." Rabbit glared at him. "I don't."

"Any honey, then?" Pooh asked hopefully.

Rabbit shook his head. "You ate all of my honey this morning, remember?"

"Oh, yes!" Pooh smiled at the memory. "It was delicious."

"Now I don't have any soup left to share with Kanga," Rabbit complained. "Why, oh, why are pooh bears always so hungry?"

"I don't know, Rabbit," Pooh said.

Piglet spoke up uncertainly. "Perhaps you could make some more soup."

"I suppose I'll have to do just that." Rabbit led the way out to his vegetable patch.

"It's a bother, no question about it," Eeyore said. "Now you'll have to spend hours picking, chopping and stirring. Such a chore. Really not many worse ways to pass a day when you think about it."

"Making soup is a chore," Rabbit agreed. "But it's certainly not the worst way to pass a day." He picked a squash.

"**First,** I get to spend time out in the sunshine selecting just the right vegetables....

Then there's the pleasant exercise of chopping and stirring....

And finally, the satisfaction of tasting the result."

Rabbit smiled. "Eeyore, you reminded me that making soup is one of my favourite ways to spend the day. Thank you!"

"Perhaps we should stay and help," Pooh said hopefully.

Rabbit's smile wavered slightly. "Er, perhaps you'd all better move along now," he said. "I need room to work."

Rabbit shooed Eeyore, Piglet and Pooh out of his garden.

"Oh, well," Eeyore said with a sigh. "I s'pose there's nothing to do now but stand here and stare at nothing."

"Don't be silly, Eeyore," Pooh said. "We should go and tell Kanga that Rabbit's making her some soup." He patted his tummy. "Perhaps she'll be so grateful that she'll insist we come in for a smackerel of honey."

They walked to the house where Kanga lived with little Roo.

When they got there, Roo was outside looking rather glum.

"What's the matter, Roo?" Piglet asked.

"He's probably worried about the storm," Eeyore suggested.

Roo looked confused. "What storm?" he asked.

"Eeyore thinks it's going to rain," Pooh explained.

"Mark my words." Eeyore cast a gloomy eye skyward.

"The rain's coming. It always does, sooner or later."

"That's not why I'm upset," Roo said. "Mama says I need
to take a bath today. And I don't like baths!"

"But why not, Roo?" Piglet exclaimed. "Baths are such a fine way of keeping clean!"

Roo crossed his arms and pouted. "I don't care about being clean. And it hurts when Mama scrubs my ears too hard."

"Hmm," Pooh said. "I see what you mean. But it can be very pleasant to sit in the warm water and think about nothing for a while. I always find it whets the appetite."

"I don't care about that, either," Roo said. "I'd much rather spend my time playing."

Eeyore spoke up. "I understand, Roo. I'm not much for bathing either. Don't really see the point."

"Really?" Piglet said. "But then how do you get clean?"

Eeyore shrugged. "Why bother getting clean?" he said. "After all, you end up getting dirty again soon enough. Might as well save the bother and just stay dirty in the first place."

"That's what I said!" Roo cried. "But Mama won't listen!"

Roo thought about what Eeyore had said. "Then again," he said, "getting dirty is an awful lot of fun."

"Is it?" Eeyore said. "I wouldn't know. I'm not very good at having fun. Never quite got the hang of it somehow. Probably my own fault. Most things are."

"It's lots of fun **rolling** in the sandpit and making mud pies," Roo said. "I love getting dirty! But you can't get dirty if you're already dirty."

Pooh scratched his head. "You can't?"

Roo laughed. "No, Pooh, you can't! I'd hate to miss all that fun by not getting clean! I can't wait for my bath!"

Just then Kanga came outside. "All right, Roo," she said.
"It's time for your bath."

"Hooray!"

Roo cheered.

He **hopped** over and **splashed!** right into the tub.

Kanga looked surprised. "Oh, my!" she said. "What's made you so cheerful about your bath today, Roo?"

Roo giggled. "It was Eeyore!" he exclaimed. "He helped me see how important a bath can be!"

Kanga smiled at Eeyore. "Thank you," she said. "It can be so difficult to get Roo into his bath."

"Eeyore's been helping others all day," Pooh said.

Piglet nodded. "He's probably the most helpful friend in the Hundred-Acre Wood!"

"I am?" Eeyore blinked dubiously. Could he really be as helpful as his friends said? "Seems unlikely," he muttered to himself. "More likely they're all soft in the head." He thought about that. "Yes, seems quite likely that's the answer. But then again, who knows? Certainly not me."

Eeyore said goodbye to his friends and wandered home, pondering all that had happened that day.

He sat down by his house and thought about it for another hour or two. Finally he was interrupted by a raindrop falling on to his head.

Then another and another.

"I knew it," he said with as much satisfaction as a gloomy creature can have. "I may not be helpful about much. But when I say it's going to rain, it always does. Sooner or later."

Hide and Pooh Seek

It was a lovely spring day in the Hundred-Acre Wood. "A nice day like this calls for a game," Christopher Robin declared.

"A game? What sort of game?" asked Winnie the Pooh.

Christopher Robin smiled. "Let's play hide-and-seek!"

Eeyore was doubtful. "And then we all fall asleep?"

Christopher Robin laughed. "Of course not! When the seeker gets to one hundred, he starts searching for the hiders."

"Hide and what now?" Rabbit asked.

"One of us closes his eyes and counts to one hundred," Christopher Robin repeated. "Meanwhile, the rest of us hide."

"I see," Pooh said, though he wasn't quite sure he did. "I suppose it's similar to how I have to search for honey whenever I run out." He rubbed his tummy. "That happens quite a bit," he admitted.

Christopher Robin tugged gently on Pooh's ear. "Tag – you're It, Pooh Bear!"

Pooh rubbed his ear. "What is it that I am, exactly?"

Now, Pooh was a Bear-of-Very-Little-Brain. But he soon figured out what was happening. He was supposed to cover his eyes, count to one hundred and then find his friends.

"One," Pooh began confidently.

Then he stopped. What came after one? He sat down to think about it.

Think, think, think ... Pooh tried to remember every
number he knew.

"Six?" he tried next. "Er, twenty-seven and a half?"

Pooh smiled. He was better at counting than he'd thought!

"Eleventy-four!" he announced.

He stopped again. That hadn't sounded quite right.

"Never mind," he said aloud to himself. "I'm sure I got most
of them." He cleared his throat. "One hundred!" he called out.
"Ready or not, here I come!"

Pooh set out to find his friends. Where could they be hiding? The answer came to him almost immediately.

"I know the perfect hiding place," he said, licking his lips hungrily. "The honey tree!"

He rushed to the honey tree.

"Aha! Found you!" he cried.

Pooh looked around in surprise. The honey tree was there. The bees were there. The honey was there, too. But there was no sign of his friends!

Pooh thought about giving up and helping himself to some honey. But then he realized where the others must be.

"If they're not here," he exclaimed, "why, then they *must* be hiding in Rabbit's garden!"

But Pooh's friends weren't
hiding in Rabbit's garden.

They also weren't in Pooh's favourite
place in the meadow where he liked to lie
and watch the clouds.

Or in his comfy bed.

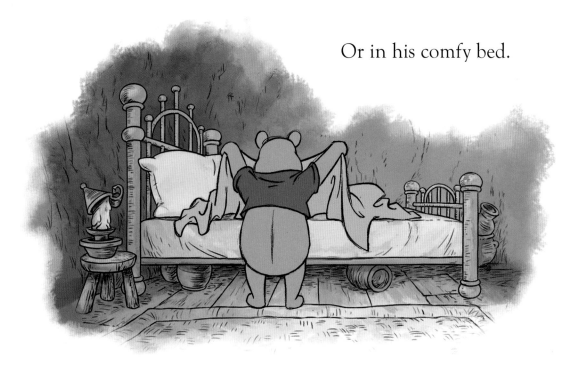

Or even at his Thoughtful Spot. "Oh, bother!" Pooh said.

Pooh did what he always did when he had a sticky problem to solve. He sat down to think.

"Think, think, think," he muttered. "Why can't I find them?"

He didn't understand it at all. Why weren't his friends hiding in any of his favourite places?

Just then Kanga came by. "Do you know where Roo is, Pooh?" she asked.

"Well, I know where he's not," Pooh said. "He's not in any of my favourite spots."

Kanga chuckled. "That's no surprise," she said kindly. "Roo has lots of his own favourite spots."

Pooh realized Kanga was right. He'd searched his favourite places. But if he wanted to find his friends, he had to check *their* favourite places!

"Think, think, think," Pooh told himself.
"Where would my friends like to hide?"

He thought about his friend Piglet.

"Piglet is a very small animal," he said. "So I
suppose he would hide in a very small spot."

Pooh thought of the smallest place he knew....

Pooh went straight to the hollow log near Piglet's house. He peered inside – and there was Piglet!

"I'm glad you found me, Pooh," Piglet admitted. "It's awfully dark in here."

"Will you help me find the others?" Pooh asked. "Let's figure out where Roo might like to hide."

Together, Pooh and Piglet found Roo
hiding – and playing – in the sandpit.

They all figured out that Tigger might be hiding in
his favourite bouncing spot.

Then they found Rabbit in his cornfield, picking corn while he hid there.

Eeyore was in his favourite thistle patch. Owl was there, too.

"I must finish my story later," Owl told Eeyore as they joined the others.

"Yes, I suppose you must," Eeyore said with a sigh.

Finally, only Christopher Robin was missing.

"Oh, dear," Piglet said. "What if we never find him?"

"We probably won't," Eeyore said, sounding gloomy.

Then Pooh remembered something.
"Christopher Robin likes to climb trees,"
he said. "Let's look ... up!"

They all looked up. "There he is!"
Roo cried. "You were right, Pooh!"

Christopher Robin climbed down from his hiding spot.

"Well done, Pooh Bear," he said. "How did you find us all

so quickly?"

Pooh shrugged. "It was easy once Kanga reminded me to search in *your* favourite spots instead of mine."

"Let's play again," Roo cried. "This time, Piglet's It!"

"One ... sixteen ... nine ..."

As Piglet began counting, the others all hurried off to find hiding places.

"Where are you going to hide, Pooh?" Christopher Robin asked.

"The honey tree, of course," Pooh said. "Piglet will know exactly where to find me."

Christopher Robin laughed. "Silly old bear!"

Piglet the Brave

Piglet was a very small animal. Almost everything in the Hundred-Acre Wood was larger than he was. Being so small could make the whole world seem rather scary at times.

Piglet was **frightened** by many things.

Dark and **spooky** shadows.

Thud!

Startling surprises.

CRASH!

BANG!

BOOM!

Loud and ANGRY thunderstorms.

Being **all** alone.

Sometimes Piglet even felt frightened in his own cosy bed. One **dark** night he had an especially scary dream. In the dream, he was collecting haycorns. All of a sudden, a haycorn fell on his head. Piglet jumped.

"Oh! You startled me!" he cried.

"How could you be scared of a tiny haycorn like me?" the haycorn asked.

Now Piglet was even more surprised. "I didn't think haycorns could talk!" he exclaimed.

"Of course we can!" a much louder voice said.

Piglet spun round and gasped. He was surrounded by
giant haycorns!

"We're going to get you, tiny Piglet!" one of the giant
haycorns growled.

BOOM!

BOOM!

"Nooooo!" Piglet cried. He began to run. The haycorns chased him. Their shadows loomed over him as thunder boomed overhead. They chased him through the Wood.

Just as Piglet thought he had managed to escape them ...

"Good morning, Piglet!" a giant haycorn called out.

"Aaaaaaaah!" Piglet screamed in terror.

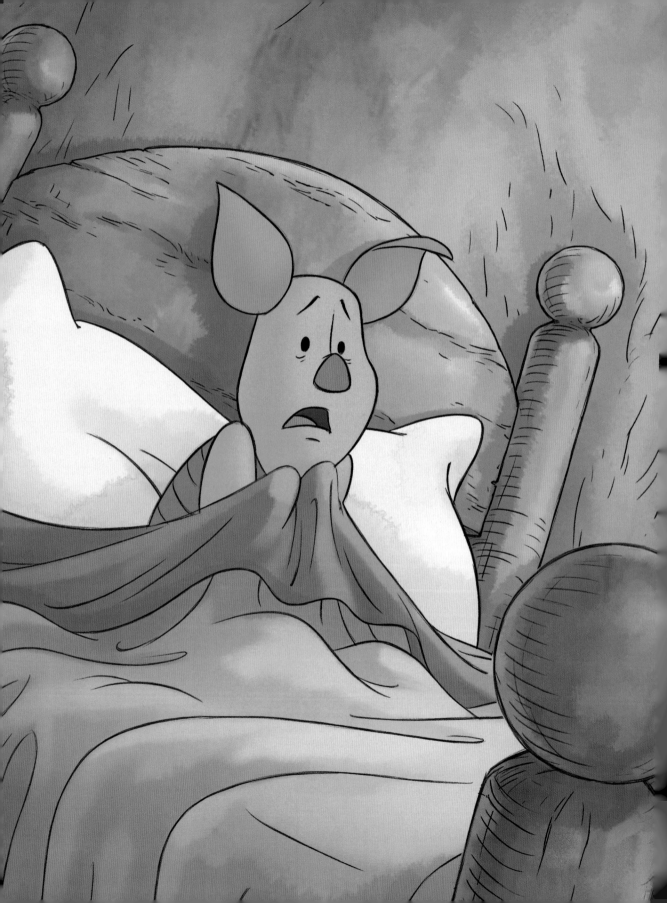

"Piglet?" the haycorn said. "Are you all right?"

Piglet opened his eyes. It wasn't a haycorn that had spoken after all! It was his friend Winnie the Pooh.

"Pooh!" Piglet gasped. "I seem to have had a bad dream."

"Oh, dear," Pooh said. "I've had those myself. Mostly about running out of honey." He shuddered.

"How do you make yourself feel better after a scary dream?" Piglet asked.

Pooh scratched his head. "I don't know," he said. "I suppose I just don't think about it."

"Oh! I'll try that then." Piglet tried not to think about his dream. But the more he tried NOT to think about it, the more he DID think about it!

"Oh, dear," Piglet said. "It's not working."

"What's not working?" Pooh asked.

"Not thinking about my scary dream," Piglet said.

"Oh, that. I'd already stopped thinking about it." Pooh thoughtfully licked some honey off his paw. "Perhaps we should ask Kanga what to do. She tends to know a great deal about this sort of thing."

So the two friends set off for Kanga's house. The path led them through the dark wood, where the tall trees cast **spooky** shadows over everything.

"Oh, d-d-dear," Piglet murmured anxiously.

He was relieved when they arrived at Kanga's house.

Little Roo was playing outside.

"Hello," Roo said. "Did you come to play with me?"

"Not exactly," Pooh said. "We came to ask Kanga how to stop Piglet from being frightened by his bad dreams."

"And by sh-sh-shadows," Piglet added, glancing back to make sure the scary shadows hadn't followed them.

"I used to be afraid of shadows, too," Roo said. "But Mama told me to use my imagination to change them from something scary into something fun."

"Fun?" Piglet shuddered. "How could you do that?"

"By playing make-believe! I'll show you!" Roo offered.

He led Piglet and Pooh into the woods. The shadows were
as dark and spooky as ever. "Now what?" asked Pooh.

"Now I pretend that the shadows are something else."
Roo thought for a second. "I know! I'm gonna pretend that
shadow there is a kite!"

Roo began pretending to fly his make-believe kite. "Look how high my kite can fly!" he cried, hopping along the path with glee.

"Hmm," Pooh said thoughtfully. "I believe I'll play make-believe with the shadows, too." He looked this way and that until he spotted a rather roundish shadow that resembled something dear to Pooh's heart ... a GIANT honeypot!

"Try it, Piglet!" Roo called cheerfully. "You'll like it!"

Piglet took a deep breath and thought about things that made him happy. As he did, a shadow beside him suddenly turned into his friend B'loon! Piglet grabbed B'loon's string and together they floated through the Wood.

"This *is* fun!" Piglet exclaimed.

Suddenly, a GIANT monster leaped into view.

"Hallooo, Pigalet!" the monster exclaimed. Only it wasn't a monster at all. It was Tigger.

"Tigger!" Piglet said. "You f-f-f-frightened me!"

"Sorry about that, Piglet Ol' Pal." Tigger said. "I'd better un-frighten you, then!"

"What was it that was so frightening *exac-ta-ly?*" Tigger

asked. "Was it my stripes? My whiskers? My *grr?*" He let out

a loud Grrr! "It was probably my *grr,* wasn't it?"

"No," Piglet said. "I mean, your *grr* is quite impressive,

Tigger. But what scared me was the surprise."

"I see," Tigger said. "Well, there's one way to fix that."

"By not surprising me any more?" Piglet asked.

"Nope!" Tigger shook his head.

"By surprising you MORE!"

Piglet was confused. "How will that help me be less scared?"

"You'll see. Now take a walk through the Wood, and I'll start surprisin' ya!"

Piglet, Pooh and Roo started walking. Tigger disappeared.
A moment later, he **bounced** Piglet off his feet again.

"Surprise!" he cried. "Are you scared?"

Piglet smiled. "No. You told me you were going to surprise
me, so I wasn't scared at all." He gasped. "Oh! It worked!"

"Told ya so," Tigger said proudly.

Just then, Kanga came into view. "It's time for your bath, Roo,"
she said. "There's a storm coming, so we must hurry!"

"A s-s-storm?" Piglet looked up. Sure enough, ANGRY black
storm clouds were gathering overhead.

When Piglet looked around, he realized he'd been left behind. "Oh, d-d-dear," he murmured.

He began to run after the others, but he froze with fear when he heard footsteps behind him.

When he saw that the footsteps belonged to Eeyore, Piglet gasped with relief. "Mercy me. You frightened me, Eeyore."

"Sorry," Eeyore said gloomily. "I can go away if you like."

"No!" Piglet said quickly. "I'd rather have the company. Being alone can be frightening."

"I suppose so," Eeyore said. "Always found it rather lonely myself. Not that I'm not used to being lonely." He sighed.

Just then, a large raindrop splashed on to Piglet's head, making him jump.

Splash!

Splash!

Splash!

Another splashed into Eeyore's eye, making him blink. Then there was a rumble of thunder.

"Oh, d-d-dear," Piglet said, feeling frightened once again. "It seems the storm is here!"

Soon, the thunder was crashing and the rain was splashing. Piglet and Eeyore huddled together under a tree.

"Well, I'm glad we're not alone in this storm," Piglet said to Eeyore. "Are you very afraid, Eeyore?"

Eeyore looked at Piglet. "I suppose I am a little," he said. "Mostly just wet, though."

Suddenly, Piglet had a thought. "Let's run to Kanga's house!"

The storm was so scary that Piglet didn't really want to leave

the shelter of the tree. But knowing that Eeyore was frightened, too,

somehow made him feel braver.

"Come on, Eeyore!" Piglet shouted.

Eeyore looked dubious. "Are you sure that's a good idea?"

"Don't be scared, Eeyore," Piglet said. "Just follow me!"

Then he dived out into the storm.

With Piglet bravely leading the way, the two friends soon made it safe and sound to Kanga's warm and cosy kitchen.

"What a terrible storm!" Piglet exclaimed.

Pooh nodded, shivering a little. "Are you still scared, Piglet?"

Piglet thought about it and then smiled. "I'm still a very small animal who isn't particularly brave," he said. "But today my friends helped me see that scary things aren't nearly as scary when you have such good friends to be brave with."

The Pooh Sticks Game

It had been a particularly windy night in the Hundred-Acre Wood. So windy in fact, that when Eeyore opened his eyes the next morning, he found himself looking up at the sky. The wind had brought his house of sticks down on top of him.

"Guess it's time to rebuild – again," said Eeyore, rolling on to his feet. Sticks Clattered noisily to the ground around him.

Eeyore had just moved all the sticks into a nice tidy pile, when Pooh and Piglet happened by on their morning walk.

Once the friends had greeted one another, Pooh took a good look at the pile. "Why, Eeyore," he said, "I see you've changed your house. Where, may I ask, is the front door? Or the back door, for that matter?"

"They're in there somewhere," replied Eeyore, who then explained what had happened.

"We'd be happy to help you rebuild your house, wouldn't we,
Pooh?" said Piglet.

"Indeed we would," said Pooh. He picked up a stick.

Eeyore shook his head. "Those sticks don't want to stick
together any more," he said. "It's time to get some new ones."

Pooh scratched his head with the stick he was still holding.
Suddenly the Bear of Little Brain had a big idea.

"Eeyore," he said, "if you have no further use for these sticks,
I believe I know something they'd be good for. A game of
Pooh Sticks!"

"Pooh Sticks!" said Piglet, clapping his hands. It had been a long time since the friends had played this game. In Pooh Sticks, several players each drop a stick over one side of the bridge and into the water. The one whose stick emerges first from under the other side of the bridge is declared the winner.

"And after the game, we'll all help you build a brand-new house," added Pooh.

Eeyore agreed and even offered to bring the sticks to the bridge. Pooh and Piglet hurried off to round up the others. Soon Pooh, Piglet, Tigger, Rabbit, Owl, Kanga, Roo and Christopher Robin had all gathered at the bridge to play.

Eeyore arrived with the sticks and was surprised to see all his friends there. But as Eeyore walked over to join them, he didn't see how close he was to the bank of the stream until ...

Splash!

Everyone hurried to look over the bridge. "Are you all right, dear?" called Kanga.

"Don't worry about me; I'll be fine," said Eeyore as he floated underneath the bridge.

Everyone ran to the other side of the bridge. Eeyore eventually emerged, followed by a number of sticks.

"Eeyore, you won!" shouted Roo. "You came out the other side first."

"Somehow it doesn't seem fair," said Eeyore, who continued to float downstream.

"Well, of course it isn't fair!" said Rabbit, annoyed. "We didn't even get a chance to pick our sticks."

It took quite a bit of doing, but Eeyore managed to make
it back to the bridge with the sticks. Eager to get the game
underway, everyone grabbed a stick and ran to one side of the
bridge. They jostled for a place at the rail and all threw their
sticks in at once. Then they hurried to the other side.

The first stick fl^oated out after just a few moments.

"That's mine!" cried Tigger with an excited bounce.

"Pooh Sticks is what tiggers do best!"

"Oh, I thought that was mine," said Roo, confused.

"Why, it looks just like the stick I picked," said Owl.

"I picked the one that looked most like my pointer."

"Nonsense! That is most certainly the stick I chose," declared Rabbit.

Everyone was rather certain that the winning stick was the one they had chosen ... until more sticks began to emerge. All the sticks looked so much alike, no one could tell who had won!

"It could just be me," said Eeyore,
"but this game isn't as much
fun as I remember."

"I think," said Christopher Robin, "that there are too
many of us playing at the same time. Maybe we should take
turns, like we used to do."

"Take turns instead of sticks?" said Eeyore. "I don't
remember that."

"No, no." Christopher Robin hurried to explain. "Take turns with the sticks. Not everyone all at once." He looked at the sticks. They all looked the same. "We need to mark these sticks somehow, so we know whose is whose."

"I have just the thing for that!" cried Piglet, who hurried off and returned with his paints. "Everyone should paint their stick so they can recognize it. I'll paint mine yellow!"

"Splendid idea, Piglet!" said Owl, who painted his stick green like the leaves of his tree home.

Tigger painted black and orange stripes down his stick. Rabbit made his entire stick orange to resemble a carrot.

Kanga painted hers pink. Roo chose blue to match his shirt. Pooh picked red for the same reason.

Christopher Robin painted the tip of his white and Eeyore chose grey, just because.

While the paint was drying, the friends agreed on some rules. Three of them would play at a time. The winner of each game would advance to the final round. The winner of that round would be the big winner! Everyone thought that not only sounded fair, but fun, too.

It was decided that Pooh should be in the first group of three, since playing Pooh Sticks had been his idea. Pooh asked Eeyore to be in the first group, too, since the sticks were from Eeyore's house, but Eeyore declined. He felt more comfortable, somehow, playing at the end.

Everyone gathered into groups of three. Pooh stepped up to the railing with Roo and Piglet. "Ready, steady, throw!" called Rabbit.

Three sticks went into the water and floated under the bridge.

PLUNK! PLINK!

PLONK!

After a few moments, a red stick came out.

"Hooray, Pooh! It's you!"

cried Piglet, pleased for his friend.

Roo was happy, too. It had been fun enough just to play.

Next, Kanga, Rabbit and Owl lined up and waited for
Christopher Robin to give them the signal to drop their sticks.
Kanga dropped hers with a flick of her wrist. Rabbit threw
his quite hard, and Owl released his as gently as
if he were shedding a feather.

They hurried to the other side, just in time to see Kanga's pretty pink stick emerge.

Everyone
cheered!

Winnie the Pooh Tales of Adventure Treasury

Christopher Robin, Tigger and Eeyore were the last three to play. "On the count of three," said Owl.

"ONE …
one and a half …
TWO …
two and three-eighths …
THREE!"

Christopher Robin let his *stick roll off his palm.*

Tigger **dropped** his mid-bounce.

Eeyore did a **twitchy** move and opened his mouth to release his stick.

Eeyore's **twitchy** move worked. He won his round! "Didn't expect that," he said, with the tiniest hint of a smile.

Everyone was so excited, they couldn't wait for the final round to begin! Pooh, Kanga and Eeyore wished each other good luck.

Piglet waved a leaf as a signal to start.

PLUNK!

PLINK!

PLONK!

Three Pooh Sticks went into the water and disappeared under the bridge.

A lone grey stick floated forward in first place. Eeyore could hardly believe his eyes.

"Hooray for Eeyore!" everyone shouted at once. "You won!"

"Must be a mistake," said the disbelieving donkey.

"No, Eeyore," Christopher Robin laughed. "We followed the rules and took turns. It's no mistake! You won fair and square!"

"Taking turns?" said Eeyore. "Who knew?" Just then, he remembered that he still needed a house. He turned to go.

"Wait for us, Eeyore!" said Pooh. "We're still going to help you build your house."

Eeyore looked back at his friends. "You are?" he asked.

"We can take turns adding sticks to it," said Roo excitedly.

"Because that's what good friends do!" said Christopher Robin.

SPOOKY
FOREST

100. AKER
WOOD

KANGAS
HOUSE

RABBITS
FRENDS AND
RALETIONS

MR SANDERZ

POOH BEARS HOUSE

SIX PINE
TREES

DRAWN BY ME